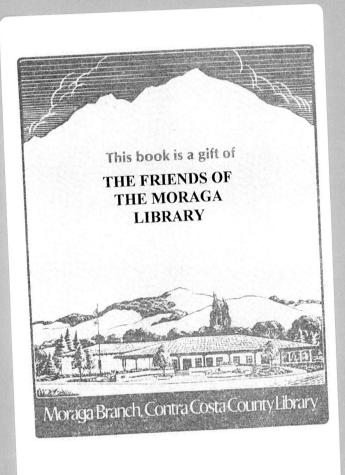

ONCE UPON A SATURDAY

Leslie Lammle

HarperCollins*Publishers*

Library of Congress Cataloging-in-Publication Data is available.

ISBN 978-0-06-125190-0 (trade bdg.) — ISBN 978-0-06-125191-7 (lib. bdg.)

Typography by Rachel Zegar

1 2 3 4 5 6 7 8 9 10

❖

First Edition

For Mom, Suzanne, David, and Wayne

ONCE UPON A SATURDAY
morning, June woke up early.

Perhaps she would search for wild animals . . .

or maybe learn how to fly . . .

or maybe even discover long-lost treasure.

Except
for one
BIG
problem:

THE LIST. June had to complete everything on it before she could play.

The more she looked at the list, the longer it appeared.

As she grumbled to herself, "WHEN WILL I GET TO DO WHAT I WANT?"

she heard her mother.

"Well, I hope it's pancakes."

"Oatmeal?" June sighed.
"Look at these lumps!"

She pulled the bowl nearer . . .

HMPH?!!

. . .to take a better look.

"AGHHH!" She gasped.
"Something is not right!"

OUT!
OUT! OUT! OUT!
I HAVE A **LONG** LIST OF THINGS TO DO THIS MORNING, AND **YOU** ARE IN THE WAY!

June shared a few choice lumps with the dog and ate the rest. Then she headed toward the front door, ready for the first chore.

As June gazed toward the mailbox, she noticed a crow flying overhead.

The closer she got,

the larger it appeared.

Happy to help, the crow flew up into
the sky and chose the shortest path.
June did her best to keep up.

She did not stop until the mail was delivered.

June lingered a moment to catch her breath,
then ran outside for the next chore.

She began to sweep. Leaves covered every step.
A little breeze tossed some of them . . .   into the garden.

"HEY!
EXCUSE ME!
MORE, PLEASE!"

WHO, ME? whistled the wind, blowing so loudly that it was difficult to hear her request.

Eager to help, the wind exhaled a strong gust that sent everything tumbling across the lawn. June shut her eyes and gripped the rail for as long as she could.

She did not open her eyes until she heard,

"Oh no. There's just one last thing to do."
June sighed and ran back up the spotless
stairs to the house.

June stood outside her room and peered in.
She watched for any movement under the bed.

She waited . . .

and listened.

PHEW! June said. "Not one monster." She recognized every single one of her missing toys.

She sorted and stored and
picked up every last one.

At last June was finished. She ran down the stairs and

opened the front door. She paused
and wondered what to do first.

She was ready to
begin her day.